A Note to Parents

Welcome to REAL KIDS READERS, a series of phonics-based books for children who are beginning to read. In the classroom, educators use phonics to teach children how to sound out unfamiliar words, providing a firm foundation for reading skills. At home, you can use REAL KIDS READERS to reinforce and build on that foundation, because the books follow the same basic phonic guidelines that children learn in school.

Of course the best way to help your child become a good reader is to make the experience fun—and REAL KIDS READERS do that, too. With their realistic story lines and lively characters, the books engage children's imaginations. With their clean design and sparkling photographs, they provide picture clues that help new readers decipher the text. The combination is sure to entertain young children and make them truly want to read.

REAL KIDS READERS have been developed at three distinct levels to make it easy for children to read at their own pace.

- LEVEL 1 is for children who are just beginning to read.
- LEVEL 2 is for children who can read with help.
- LEVEL 3 is for children who can read on their own.

A controlled vocabulary provides the framework at each level. Repetition, rhyme, and humor help increase word skills. Because children can understand the words and follow the stories, they quickly develop confidence. They go back to each book again and again, increasing their proficiency and sense of accomplishment, until they're ready to move on to the next level. The result is a rich and rewarding experience that will help them develop a lifelong love of reading.

For Marie Edouard, with thanks and appreciation
—M. L.

Special thanks to Playhut Inc. for providing the tent and to
Morgenthal Frederics, New York City, for providing the eyeglasses.

Produced by DWAI / Seventeenth Street Productions, Inc.
Reading Specialist: Virginia Grant Clammer

Millbrook Press
A division of Lerner Publishing Group
241 First Avenue North
Minneapolis, MN 55401 U.S.A.

Website address: www.lernerbooks.com

Library of Congress Cataloging-in-Publication Data

Leonard, Marcia.
    My camp-out / Marcia Leonard ; photographs by Dorothy Handelman.
        p.   cm. — (Real kids readers. Level 1)
    Summary: A young girl camps out in her bedroom and is joined by her mother.
    ISBN-13: 978-0-7613-2052-4 (lib. bdg. : alk. paper)
    ISBN-10: 0-7613-2052-0 (lib. bdg. : alk. paper)
    ISBN-13: 978-0-7613-2077-7 (pbk. : alk. paper)
    ISBN-10: 0-7613-2077-6 (pbk. : alk. paper)
    [1. Camping–Fiction. 2. Mothers and daughters–Fiction. 3. Afro-Americans–Fiction.
4. Stories in rhyme.] I. Handelman, Dorothy, ill. II. Title. III. Series.
PZ8.3.L54925Mu   1999
[E]—dc21   98-38106

Manufactured in the United States of America
4 5 6 7 8 9 – DP – 10 09 08 07 06 05

My Camp-Out

By Marcia Leonard
Photographs by Dorothy Handelman

M Millbrook Press • Minneapolis

I have my tent.

5

I have my lamp.

I have my bag.

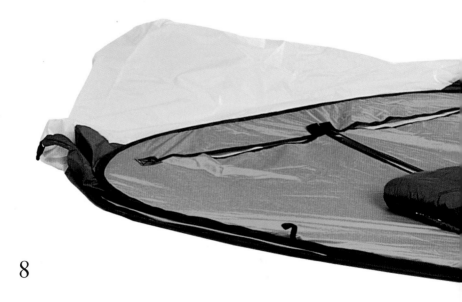

I'm set to camp.

11

My tent is up.

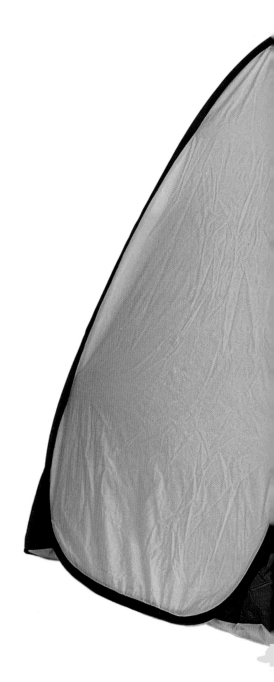

13

I make my bed.

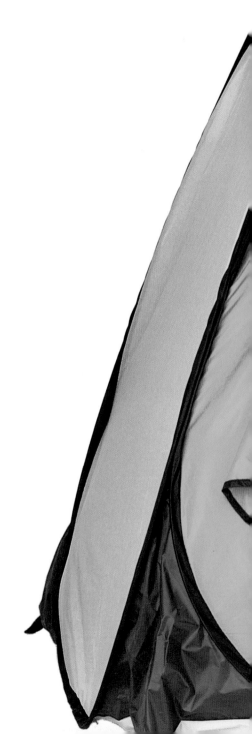

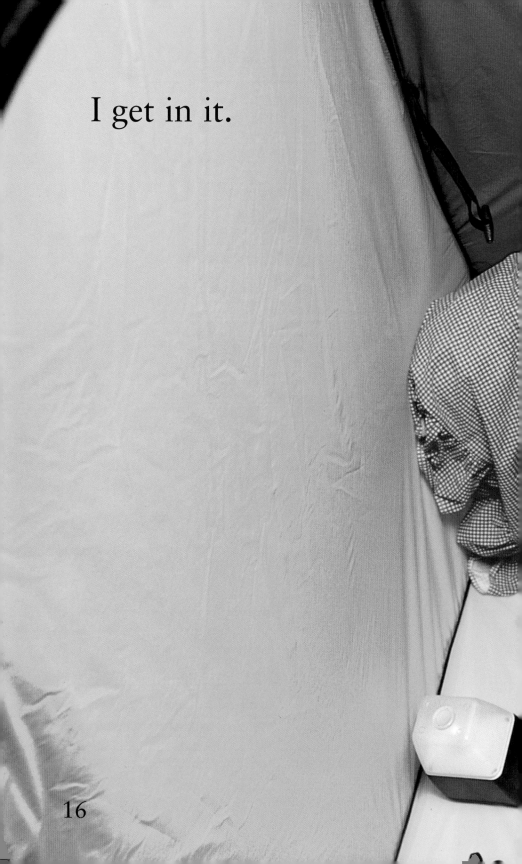

I get in it.

I rest my head.

Now it is dark.
I can't see well.

What is out there?
I can not tell.

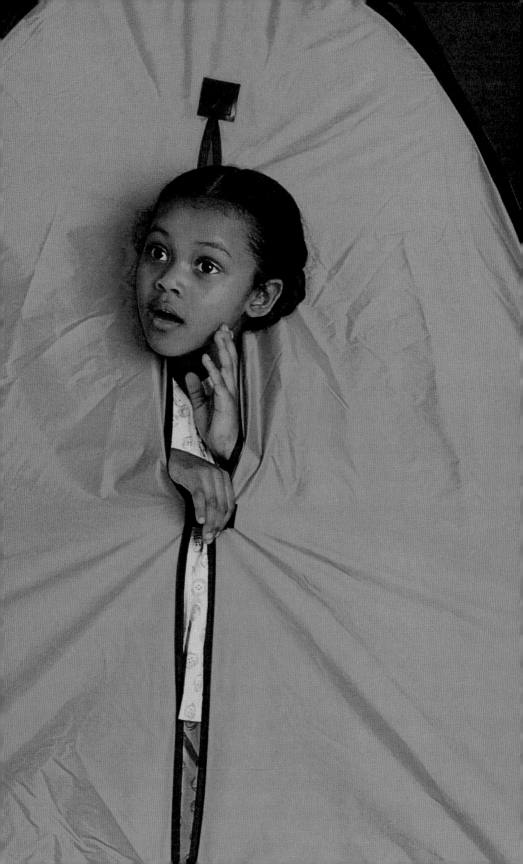

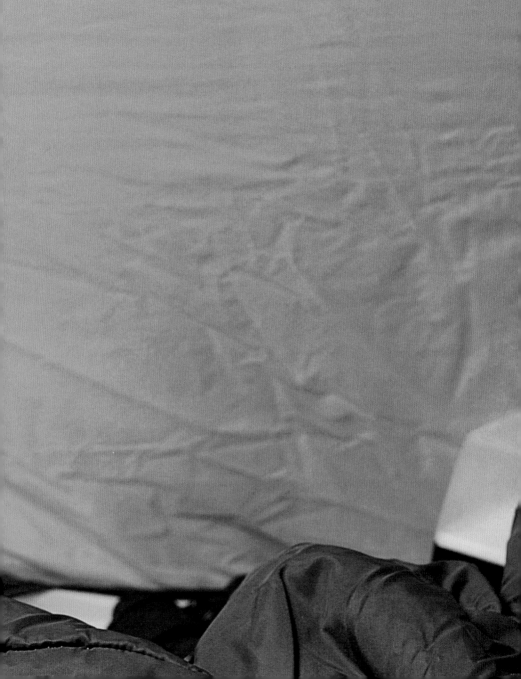

What was that bump?
Was it a cat?

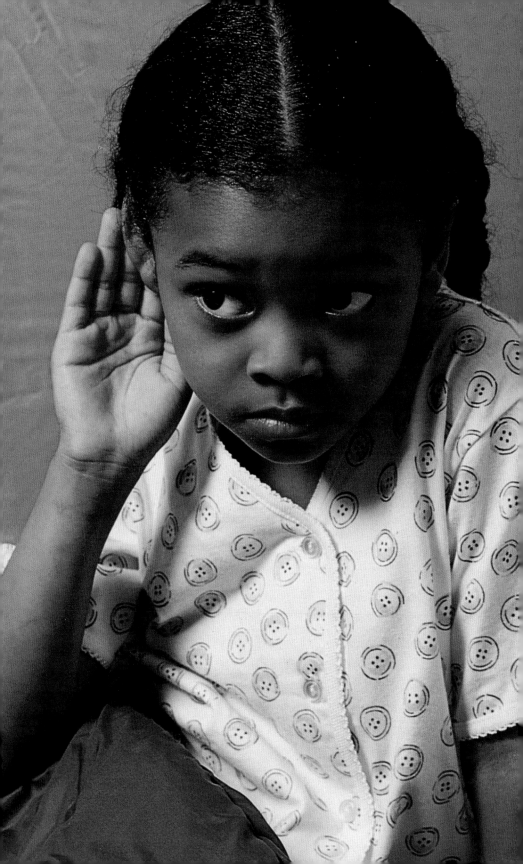

Was it a bird,
a bug, a bat?

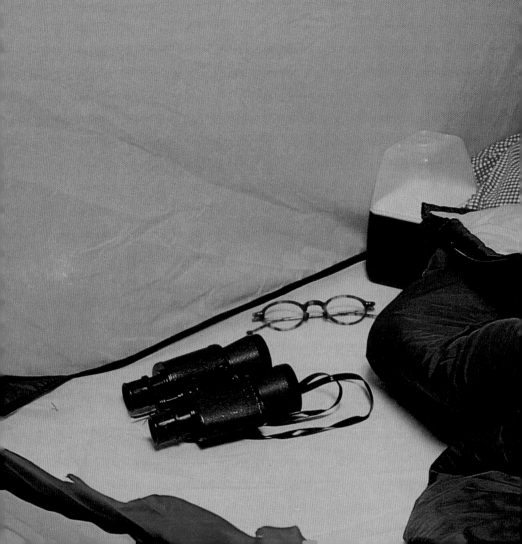

I look again.
It's Mom I see!

I am so glad
she will camp with me.

Reading with Your Child

1. Try to read with your child at least twenty minutes each day, as part of your regular routine.
2. Keep your child's books in one convenient, cozy reading spot.
3. Read and familiarize yourself with the Phonic Guidelines below.
4. Ask your child to read *My Camp-Out* out loud. If he or she has difficulty with a word:
   - Help him or her decode the word phonetically. (Say, "Try to sound it out.")
   - Encourage him or her to use picture clues. (Say, "What does the picture show?")
   - Ask him or her to use context clues. (Say, "What would make sense?")
5. If your child still doesn't "get" the word, tell him or her what it is. Don't wait for frustration to build.
6. Praise your beginning reader. With your enthusiasm and encouragement, your child will go from one success to the next.

Phonic Guidelines

Use the following guidelines to help your child read the words in *My Camp-Out*.

Short Vowels
When two consonants surround a vowel, the sound of the vowel is usually short. This means you pronounce *a* as in apple, *e* as in egg, *i* as in igloo, *o* as in octopus, and *u* as in umbrella. Short-vowel words in this story include: *bag, bat, bed, bug, can, cat, get, Mom, not, set.*

Short-Vowel Words with Beginning Consonant Blends
When two different consonants begin a word, they usually blend to make a combined sound. A word in this story with a beginning consonant blend is *glad.*

Short-Vowel Words with Ending Consonant Blends
When two different consonants end a word, they usually blend to make a combined sound. Words in this story with ending consonant blends include: *bump, camp, dark, lamp, rest, tent.*

R-Controlled Vowels
When a vowel is followed by the letter *r*, its sound is changed by the *r*. A word in this story with an *r*-controlled vowel is *bird.*

Double Consonants
When two identical consonants appear side by side, one of them is silent. In this story, double consonants appear in the short-vowel words *tell, well, will.*

Sight Words
Sight words are those words that a reader must learn to recognize immediately—by sight—instead of by sounding them out. They occur with high frequency in easy texts. Sight words not included in the above categories are: *a, again, am, have, I, in, is, it, look, make, my, or, out, see, she, so, that, there, to, was, what, with, up.*

REAL KIDS READERS

My Camp-Out

This girl is all set to camp out. Her tent is up. Her sleeping bag is unrolled. She's ready for a good night's sleep... but then it gets dark.

Other REAL KIDS READERS™ — Level 1:

Best Friends
Big Ben
The Big Box
Dan and Dan
Dress-Up
Get the Ball, Slim
Hop, Skip, Run
I Am Mad!
I Like Mess

I Like to Win!
Mud!
My Pal Al
The New Kid
No New Pants!
The Pet Vet
Spots
The Tin Can Man
Wash Day

Level 1: Beginning to Read
Level 2: Reading with Help
Level 3: Reading Independently

$4.99 USA
$7.99 Canada

FIRST AVENUE EDITIONS
AN IMPRINT OF LERNER PUBLISHING GROUP
www.lernerbooks.com

ISBN 0-7613-2077-6

50499

9 780761 320777

REAL KIDS READERS™

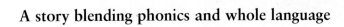

A story blending phonics and whole language

Stop That Noise!

By Margery Bernstein

Photographs by Dorothy Handelman

This book belongs to

_____

DISCARD